JUSTICE FOR JASPER

A Western Novella

A.T. BUTLER

CHAPTER ONE

Jacob Payne almost got himself bit.

"Whoa, there!" He pulled his fingers away just in time. The dapple gray mustang had seemed friendly enough, but as soon as Jacob's fingers brushed close to its mouth, it snapped at him. Jacob glared at the horse's current owner. "Thought you said this one was broken."

Caleb Shaw widened his eyes, wearing his most innocent expression. "He is. You musta riled him somehow."

"Uh huh," Jacob muttered.

He turned back to examine the horse, keeping out of reach of its strong jaw—which was no way to really learn anything, but he kept trying. Jacob needed to have something to ride out of there today.

The bounty hunter's previous horse, Paint, had

been shot from under him while he was on the trail of a bank robber out in the desert. In the several days since he captured Jed Corker and turned him over to the lawful authorities, he had managed to do without a horse of his own, staying in town and going everywhere on foot.

But now, looking at Shaw's meager selection, Jacob wondered how much longer he could do without. It's not that he couldn't afford a fine horse, but more that there were none to be had. His current options were a mare that had given birth two days earlier, a Morgan that could not be younger than twenty years, or this one with the biting—Shaw called him Smoke. Jacob wondered how he'd manage to bridle the creature without losing his fingers.

"You sure you don't have any others for sale, Shaw?" Jacob asked, turning back to the the man.

"Payne, I swear—"

"Jacob Payne!" a big voice shouted from the doorway of the livery. "Anyone seen Payne?"

"Who's asking?" Jacob shouted back. Shielding his eyes against the sunny backdrop, Jacob made out the silhouette of a tall, thin man walking toward him. Out here in Arizona Territory, a stranger knowing his name could either be very good or very bad.

"U.S. Marshal Owen Santos," the man said as he approached.

As the stranger got closer, Jacob noticed he was

holding up a badge. From this distance he couldn't make out what the badge said, but he'd heard of Santos all right.

"I'm Jacob Payne. What can I do for you, Marshal?"

Santos took off his hat and offered his hand to the bounty hunter. The marshal stood taller than Jacob by several inches, which was uncommon, but was leaner than a bean pole. Jacob's broad shoulders could probably hide the other man behind him twice over.

He shook the marshal's hand, then noticed Shaw awkwardly watching the interaction.

"Have you met Caleb Shaw, Marshal?" he asked, gesturing.

The lawman glanced at the livery owner, barely acknowledging him before turning his attention back to Jacob. "I'm gonna tell you this straight. I need your help. I can legally force you into helping, but I'd rather you come willingly."

Jacob was half defensive and half amused by this approach. Though he wasn't technically a man of the law, he still respected what men like Santos had to do. "What is it you need, sir?"

Santos let out a deep sigh and rolled his eyes. His annoyance rolled off of him in waves. "Well, seems the sheriff down in Jasper can't do the job he was elected to do. He's called on the marshal's office for assistance, and all my men are out in the field."

"Assistance with what?"

"Claims he's identified a wanted murderer, one Floyd Daly. But seeing as the man is currently in the employ of the Rockville Mining Company, he's having a devil of a time even getting close to him."

"You need me to go down and capture this Daly character?"

"Oh, I don't mind goin' down there to collect the man myself, but I don't dare trust the sheriff to back me up if I need it. I need a capable associate by my side if things go south. You're the first person I thought of."

"Why me?"

"All I been hearin' these last few months is 'Jacob Payne *this*' and 'Jacob Payne *that*.' You've made quite the impression since you arrived in Arizona. Bonnie, in particular, seems to like the taste of your name in her mouth."

Jacob smiled. Bonnie, his favorite waitress at the San Xavier Cafe just a few blocks away, sure did make his visits to Tucson pleasant. But she couldn't be the only one talking about him to the U.S. Marshal. Likely the sheriffs of Bennettsville or Valleseco—or maybe even San Adrian, if they had a new sheriff already—would be speaking well of him.

"I'm happy to help if I can, Marshal."

"Much obliged. I'll deputize you now and we'll be on our way tomorrow morning."

"One problem, sir. I still don't have a horse—"

"Since Jed Corker shot yours? Yeah, I heard about that, too. Hanging's too good for that one, I tell you. Well, fine." Santos looked around the stable for the first time. "None of these?"

Jacob hesitated. "I was hoping to be able to invest in a more reliable animal."

Santos nodded. "I see." He glared at Caleb. "Well, in that case, just leave it to me. I'll find a mount for you by tomorrow. You can't get the thing killed, though."

"I'll do my best," Jacob said with a grin. "You have any idea why the sheriff down in Jasper can't get his man?"

Santos sighed. "Like I said—Daly managed to get a job working at the Vernon Copper Mine and has apparently made himself indispensable. The boss always has some excuse why he can't be bothered or why they can't reveal his whereabouts."

"All right." Jacob considered what kind of security might be around a mine. "We'll find a way to get to him."

"Damn right, we will," Santos said vehemently. "Glad you'll be joining me, Payne. Come on over to my office. We got a lot to do."

He led the way out of the livery.

"So you won't be taking Smoke?" Caleb asked before Jacob left.

The bounty hunter looked at the other man, exasperated. "The horse that almost *bit* me? No, Caleb. Not this time."

Caleb nodded, while Jacob hurried to catch up with Santos and prepare to track down the outlaw Daly.

CHAPTER TWO

The ride south to Jasper took two full days, the marshal cursing the town's sheriff the whole time. The horse Santos had rounded up for Jacob before they left Tucson was sufficient, though nothing to get all that excited about.

"His name is Yellow," Santos had said when he met Jacob outside his hotel at dawn. "He belongs to my neighbor. I told him we'd be back within the week."

Jacob approached Yellow, letting the animal smell him before he climbed on. "Hey there, boy."

He pet the animal's long neck and shoulder. The horse was a deep chestnut brown with white stockings on its two front feet. It was alert and gentle. But one thing it was not was yellow.

"Yellow, huh? Please tell me he's not called that on account of his lack of courage."

Santos laughed. "I couldn't say. I guess we'll find out."

Jacob grinned. At least the animal didn't bite. "Okay, Yellow. You and me, huh?" The horse nuzzled his ear. "Yeah, I think we'll get along just fine, Marshal."

"Glad to hear it, seeing as we don't have any other options. Let's get moving. I'd like to get as far as we can before dark."

Now, more than thirty hours later, Jacob and Yellow followed closely behind Santos and his horse as they crossed over into the outskirts of Jasper.

This was Jacob's first visit to the town, but Santos had filled him in on the history. The town had been built up around the Vernon Copper Mine, which was run by the Rockville Mining Company. When copper was discovered there three years ago, the Vernon brothers had bought up all the claims and monopolized the area. Jasper—named after one of the brothers—was a company town, almost entirely populated by miners, with the occasional soiled dove, bartender, preacher, and a handful of other industrious business people who saw a chance to make money.

They approached Jasper from the north, through the low hills full of scrub and cactus. The first buildings they came to were seemingly abandoned boarding houses, far from the town center. Whoever lived there, likely bachelor miners, were gone for the day. Every block or so, they'd tip their hats to the women hanging clothes out to dry, hauling water, or weeding in the small dirt yards around the clapboard houses.

The street Santos led them through wound downhill, through the small residential area, until Jacob began to recognize what must be the main street of Jasper. He counted no fewer than three separate saloons within a four-block stretch and chuckled to himself. Maybe that's one of the reasons the sheriff here was having so much trouble.

"Are we going straight to the mine?" Jacob asked.

Santos reined his horse to let Jacob catch up with him. "Not just yet. It's far to the south of town. I figure we'll stop by the jail and see if the sheriff has any news for us. If not, we can get us settled in a hotel and make our assault on the mine tomorrow."

"Assault?" Jacob grinned. "You got it, boss."

"That's right—assault. Seeing as whatever pleading and reasoning Sheriff Alway has tried ain't working, that's probably the next step. If words don't work, I have no problem using my gun. Which is why I brought along my temporary deputy."

Jacob's grin widened. "Glad to be of service."

Before they began to move again, Jacob heard a plaintive voice coming from farther down the road.

"Come on, Oscar. I don't want to have to shoot you."

Santos and Jacob exchanged a quick glance

before nudging their horses ahead to wherever this Oscar person was. They turned the next right corner to find a portly man, who could only be the sheriff with that gleaming badge, yanking on the arm of another man who was clearly passed out drunk in the dusty road. Even from this distance, Jacob could tell the drunk was unconscious and not able to even hear the sheriff's commands, let alone follow them.

"Oscar, I done told you and told you. Destroying Miss Jessie's property is grounds for arrest. You're gonna have to spend the night in the jail, so let's get you there."

He yanked again, the other man's dead weight barely moving a couple inches. The sheriff dropped the limp arm to the ground and fumbled for his gun.

"Sheriff," Santos called, his voice carrying across the distance. "You wouldn't be getting ready to shoot an unarmed, unconscious man, would you?"

Sheriff Alway looked up, surprised. "This man is not defenseless. He just overturned two Faro tables at Jessie's Parlor."

"That may be true, but that was then. Take a look at the man now, Sheriff." Santos dismounted and tossed his reins to Jacob. The bounty hunter watched as the marshal approached the sheriff, his right hand casually but pointedly resting on the grip of his revolver, still in its holster. "How much has this man had to drink?"

"I really couldn't say. I'm sorry, I didn't catch your name."

"I'm U.S. Marshal Owen Santos. You might recall the name, since you wired for me to come down from Tucson to save your sorry ass."

That seemed to have been a magic word. As soon as Santos announced his title, Sheriff Alway grasped his hand, pumping it up and down and all but blubbering in his joy.

"Mr. Santos! Oh, thank goodness. Yes, sir. Just as you say, I'll not be drawing a gun on"—he nudged the man at his feet—"Mr. Tunney. We'll get him nice and comfy in a jail cell where he can sleep it off."

Jacob dismounted and led the horses to where Santos was helping Alway commandeer a couple bystanders to carry the unconscious Tunney. Alway, Santos, Jacob, and their two horses followed behind two men holding up Oscar between them, crossing the street and carrying him into the Jasper jail.

As the two bystanders carried the drunken man inside, the sheriff stayed on the boardwalk and tried to get rid of the marshal and Jacob.

"You see, Mr. Santos, you've caught me at a bad time. It's a real shame I've gotta process this fella now and can't accompany you."

"It's about what we expected, Alway."

"You boys want I should make you a map to the mine office? Mr. Farnsworth is usually there all hours of night if you want to talk to him now."

"I think it's better if we head down to the mine first thing tomorrow," Santos said.

"It's getting dark," Jacob said in agreement, looking up at the sky. With Jasper situated between the hills as it was, the sun had already set half an hour earlier. The soft purple sky was quickly turning to black as stars began popping into view. "I don't want to be caught unawares. Tomorrow would be better. Let's find a place to sleep for the night."

"Just as you say. Oscar will keep a bit yet while I see to you. Come along, fellas," Sheriff Alway said. "Let's introduce you to Mrs. Courtland."

CHAPTER THREE

As they crossed the threshold into the three-story hotel built into the hill, a curvy blonde crossed the room to greet them, beaming. She wore a deceptively low-cut dress, with a filmy lace covering her decolletage.

"Abby," Sheriff Alway called. Jacob noticed he didn't bother to remove his hat. "I'd like you to take special care of these guests of mine. This here is U.S. Marshal Santos from Tucson, and his deputy Mr. Payne."

Jacob doffed his hat, bowing his head slightly as he took Mrs. Courtland's offered hand.

"Abby Courtland," she said with a dazzling, dimpled smile. As she bobbed her head, several curls fell forward into her face. She giggled, pushing them back with her free hand. "It's always a joy when the sheriff brings me guests."

"Right, well. We're mighty lucky they're here." The sheriff clapped his hand on Santos's shoulder. "I'll let you boys rest a bit and come see about breakfast in the morning. I can't tell you enough how much I appreciate you being here, Marshal."

"Our pleasure, Sheriff. We'll see you in the morning."

"I've got just the place for y'all," Mrs. Courtland said. "Come upstairs with me."

She led the way past a young girl at the foot of the stairs who tried to catch Jacob's eye. When she leaned toward him, he smiled politely but didn't turn his focus from the matter at hand. The second floor of the hotel seemed just as noisy as the saloon on the ground floor, but Mrs. Courtland kept leading them farther up into the third floor. There were fewer rooms up here, with less evidence of heavy traffic.

"No one will bother y'all up here. I hope you get a good chance to rest. Your room rate includes supper and a whiskey downstairs. I believe we're serving stew tonight. I'll go tell Wilbur to look for you," she explained as she led them down the hallway. "Here's Mr. Payne's room."

She opened the room to her right and let the door swing open, stepping back to let Jacob go in first.

"Thank you, ma'am."

She nodded. "There's a wash basin on the dresser, and an extra blanket at the foot of the bed. I'll go get

Mr. Santos settled and then come back to check on you," she said, touching his arm lightly.

Once he was left alone, Jacob tossed his bag onto the bed and looked around. The furniture was worn, scratched in some places, but solid. The floral wallpaper looked brand new. He thought about how hard it must be for Mrs. Courtland to run this business by herself, and how pleased she must have been when she had saved enough money to paper the rooms. But then, Jacob had seen many remarkable women in the west, called to do any number of remarkable things they wouldn't have even thought to do if they had stayed in the safe cities in the eastern states. Mrs. Courtland must be one of these.

He had just finished washing his face and hands for supper when he heard a light knock on the door. With a towel still in one hand, he opened the door to find his hostess standing there beaming at him. Something about her smile made Jacob feel like this woman was genuinely happy to see him, and not just pretending to be like she might for other guests.

"How is everything, Mr. Payne? I see you found the towels. Did you see there's a hook here on the back of the door for your hat or coat if you like?"

"Thank you, Mrs. Courtland. That will be mighty helpful."

"Oh, call me Abby," she said, stepping past him into the room.

Jacob opened the door wider, glancing out into the

hallway to see if anyone had seen her enter. He wouldn't want to be a reason anyone made assumptions about her.

"Well, in that case, you can call me Jacob."

She strolled a tight circle around his room, checked the dust on top of the headboard, and returned to stand near the chair at the door. "Jacob." She smiled at him over her shoulder. "Is there anything I can do for you? Any way I can make your stay more comfortable?"

"No, I don't think so. Thank you. I was just going to head down for supper."

"I could have supper brought up to you if you like." She stepped closer to him; the weight of her skirt pressed against his legs and the warmth of her body crowded around him.

"No—" Jacob cleared his throat. "No, thank you, ma'am."

"You know, Jacob . . ." She placed her hand lightly against his arm again. "The sheriff told me to make sure you're well taken care of. You sure I can't offer you some company? Doesn't have to be mine. I've got a real nice selection of girls for you to choose from."

He put his big hand over her delicate one. He liked the feel of her warm touch on his arm, but not enough to take advantage of her. "No, ma'am. I appreciate the offer. I'm sure your . . . selection is mighty fine. But I didn't come to Jasper to enjoy myself. It wouldn't be right if I was too tired tomorrow to assist the marshal."

"Why did y'all come to Jasper?" she asked after a beat. She withdrew her hand and made herself comfortable in the only chair in the room, apparently not offended by his gentle rejection of her offers.

Jacob hesitated. It didn't seem proper to sit on the bed with a lady in the room, but neither did it seem proper to stand over her. He compromised by perching himself uncomfortably on the footboard, praying it would hold under his weight.

"I'm not sure how much I'm allowed to say, ma'am."

"Abby."

"Abby. I'm not really a deputy. This is just a temporary assignment, so I'm not too sure what the rules are."

"I see."

"But, I will say that Marshal Santos and me came down here because your sheriff asked for our help capturing an outlaw."

Her expression hardened. For a fleeting moment, Jacob wondered if he had offended her somehow. And then, through clenched teeth, she said, "You wouldn't be here after Floyd Daly, would you?"

CHAPTER FOUR

Jacob gaped at the woman. "How did you— That is, I'm not supposed to say, but why do you ask about Floyd Daly?"

"Oh!" Abby looked furious. "That man is rotten to the core. He should have been brought to justice long before now. I keep telling the sheriff, but that man couldn't teach a hen to cluck. Nice enough, but *nice* don't cut it when we're dealing with a monster like Daly. I tell you what, Mr. Payne—if it *is* Floyd Daly you come down here to capture, I'll help you in any way I can. And if it's someone else, might I suggest you also look into Daly before you leave town?"

Jacob chuckled. "I might as well tell you it is Daly. I don't think the marshal would like me to be starting up a list of folk that Alway should be taking care of on his own."

"But he hasn't been. Don't you see?" She leaned

forward excitedly. "Daly may have already been a wanted man when he arrived in Jasper, but that hasn't stopped him from his despicable behavior here. He's been stealing and cheating nearly every person in this town, and Sheriff should have locked him up long ago."

"Why hasn't he?"

"Scared." She leaned back again. "Mr. Farnsworth at the mine has taken quite a shine to Daly, and Sheriff is petrified of upsetting him. The Rockville Mining Company owns this town—or most of it. Enough that Sheriff probably thinks pleasing Mr. Farnsworth is the way to get reelected."

"It's not?"

Abby shook her head. "I'm not sure, but I don't think so. There are enough business owners besides Farnsworth who want the law working the way it should that any vote would be close."

"Even if there's not, that's no reason for the sheriff to not arrest the criminal. How does Daly keep getting away with it?"

"Too many people in this town work for the mine and want to keep Mr. Farnsworth happy. I don't know why he likes Daly so much, anyway. Any criminal like that is just waiting for a chance to take in another victim. It's just a matter of time before he cheats the mining company the same way he's cheated everyone else in this town."

"I don't doubt you're right."

"If you really can bring in Daly and stop him from taking advantage of every breathin' man, woman, and child, you'll be doing the town of Jasper an enormous service. We all deserve justice same as any other town. And Sheriff Alway will be reminded of that come the next election."

A knock on Jacob's open door startled them.

"You want to head down for supper?" Santos asked. "Everything okay here? Mrs. Courtland, is my deputy bothering you?"

"Oh no, not at all." She stood and exited into the hallway. "I was just filling him in a little about Jasper and how grateful we are that you boys are here to help Sheriff Alway."

Santos looked at Jacob questioningly.

"Let's go eat. I'll give you the details," Payne muttered.

By the time they reached the saloon downstairs, Santos knew as much about what had been going on in Jasper as Jacob did. Abby found them a seat, then went to get their food.

Once she was out of earshot, Payne said, "I'm not sure an assault first thing tomorrow is the best plan, Marshal."

Abby returned carrying two glasses of whiskey, followed just behind by a girl carrying three bowls of steaming stew.

"You don't mind if I join you, do you, gentlemen?"

"Our pleasure, ma'am," Jacob said as he stood to help Abby into her chair.

"Don't let me interrupt," Abby said as she sat.

Santos nodded. "What were you saying, Payne?"

"I think we should try talking to Mr. Farnsworth first, before we try anything forceful."

"Talking?" Santos shook his head and took a bite of stew. "From what I hear, all that's been done is talking."

"That may be, but if what our host here says is true, I'm not sure we can trust Sheriff Alway's version of events. Mrs. Courtland—"

"Abby."

"—Abby. You say you know of more Jasper citizens who have been cheated by this Daly?"

She nodded vigorously. "I do. I can think of, oh, five or six right now. And I bet there's more."

"Does Mr. Farnsworth know about these other . . . indiscretions?"

Abby thought for a moment, staring into the space above Jacob's shoulder before answering. "I don't know. Could be he hasn't. I don't know anyone brave enough to tell him."

"Not even you?" Jacob teased.

"Oh, you joke, Jacob Payne, but I would march over there right now in the pitch dark if I thought it would do any good." Her dimples winked at him when she retorted.

"I do not doubt that at all. Won't be necessary, though. Not yet."

"What are you suggesting, Payne?" Santos said.

"From what we've been told, there's been a lot of talk but maybe not by the right people. If Abby can get some of the other Jasper citizens to come with us, to establish a pattern of behavior, maybe Mr. Farnsworth will see that it's in his best interest to turn over Daly to the law now, before he gets swindled himself."

Jacob took a bite of his stew and let Santos think over his proposal without pushing any further. He didn't know if his plan would work. Probably not, actually. But he hated the idea of bringing violence to the mine, of disturbing the other men's place of work —especially if it could be avoided. There would be time for that if that's what it came to, but maybe they could win over Mr. Farnsworth first.

"All right, Payne. We'll try it your way first. It can't hurt. Abby, can you gather a few of your friends, like you were saying? Meet us here right after breakfast?"

"I'll write them all notes tonight and send them with a couple of my girls. I assure you, gentlemen, Jasper is full of folk who want to see Floyd Daly brought to justice."

"I'm glad to hear it," Santos said, and Payne nodded in agreement. "Tomorrow we'll figure out how to deliver that justice."

CHAPTER FIVE

The next morning, after breakfast, Jacob and Santos walked out of Abby's hotel to find her speaking to a cluster of three men and another woman on the boardwalk. Abby seemed to be in the middle of an animated explanation when they interrupted.

"This them?" Santos asked.

"Yes, sir," Abby said, grandly gesturing. "Each of these fine citizens you see before you has been cheated, robbed, or double-crossed by Floyd Daly."

"And y'all are willing to testify to that?"

They all nodded.

"Yes, sir," the older man said. "I been waiting for a chance to say my piece."

"And you know that we're going to go talk to Mr. Farnsworth of the Rockville Mining Company before we do anything else, don't you?"

The older man frowned, and then looked back at

Abby. "Well now, Abby, you didn't say nothing about going to the mine first."

"Well . . ." She fiddled with the ruffle at the end of her sleeve. "I didn't exactly know that's what would be asked of them."

"Hmm," Santos said, frowning. "Gentlemen, ma'am. I appreciate you coming down here first thing this morning. I know you all must be very busy people. But if Mrs. Courtland here wasn't clear, let me tell you that we are planning on taking your accusations to Mr. Farnsworth. We believe—we hope—that showing him that his treasured employee has demonstrated a pattern of untrustworthy behavior will help us capture Daly without too much interruption or bloodshed."

"Oh no, I couldn't," the woman said in a whisper. "My Bill is a foreman at the mine. I couldn't—he could lose his job, and then what would we do?"

"I understand, Missus . . . ?"

"Mrs. Lennox."

"Of course. Mrs. Lennox." Santos took her hand in both of his. "We don't want to ask you to take on any risk you're not comfortable taking. Why don't you head on home today? We'll let you know if we need you to testify for a judge."

"Oh, thank you," she said, still in a whisper. She darted down the street before anyone could ask anything else of her.

"I'm not sure about this either," the older man said.

Santos waved him away without another word and turned his attention to the two remaining men, one holding a bowler hat in his hand and wearing a neat, gray jacket, the other glaring at Jacob as though he were to blame for the fact that the man was awake so early.

"And you two?" Jacob asked them.

Bowler Hat offered his hand to both lawmen to shake. "I'm Arthur Devlin. I run the general store just up the ways there." He indicated with his thumb, pointing up the street. "I'm not afraid of the mine officials. They need me to keep the wives happy with their ribbons and other doodads. Daly has run up a hell of a bill with me, and now he just laughs it off when I press him about it."

"Thank you, Mr. Devlin. I appreciate you being willing to share your experience." Jacob turned to the final man, eyebrows raised.

The glaring man spat in the dirt next to him. "Daly cheats at cards," he declared.

Santos and Jacob exchanged a look. That news seemed unsurprising.

"I'm sorry to hear that, Mister—" Jacob began.

"Sorry, nothin'." He spat again. "They call me Gentle Jack. I'm the only Gentle Jack in Jasper, and Daly'll know. He knows. He bilked me out of all of last month's pay. The man cheats."

"So this was recent?" Jacob clarified.

Gentle Jack nodded. "This last time, yeah."

"He's done this before?"

"Course he has. 'Bout every few weeks or so I fancy a game. This last time was the worst, though."

"All right," Santos said, clapping a hand on both men's shoulders. "If you two can gather your horses, my deputy and I will lead the way. We'll be able to meet with Mr. Farnsworth and bring our concerns to his attention."

"Think we should wait for the sheriff?" Jacob asked.

Santos frowned. "I doubt it. He's probably at home right now coming up with his excuses to stay in."

"Abby, will you be joining us?" Jacob asked.

"I sure will. Wilbur knows he's in charge till I get back. I can't wait to get my hands on Daly."

Jacob laughed. "How about you leave that to us?"

"We'll see," she replied darkly.

The road to the mining office was wide and well traveled. What it lacked in shade it made up for in direct, level traveling path, much different from the winding, hilly road they had entered town on.

After about a half an hour's ride, Gentle Jack pointed out a low building in the distance that looked like it was being held together with chicken wire. Jacob was pleased to see the mining official at least had no vanity or pretension in his place of business.

"That there is the offices of Rockville Mining Company," Jack said.

"And Mr. Farnsworth should be there?" Santos asked.

"As far as I've heard, he never leaves," Abby quipped.

Jacob didn't join in the conversation, keeping his attention fixed on the office building and the workers milling around it. As they got closer, he noticed that while most of the workers were going in and out of the office or working on construction nearby, there was one shadowy figure that stood around the corner of the building seemingly doing nothing. Jacob suspected that man was watching him as closely as he himself was being watched.

Jacob unhooked his hammer loop. He sat up straighter in his saddle, letting his full height and breadth be seen. Not many men would tussle willingly with Jacob Payne.

Santos led the caravan of horses to the mining office, hitching his mount to the post outside. He moved to help Abby off hers, but she had already reached the ground and waved away his offered hand.

"Mr. Santos, the only thing I need help with will be keeping my temper."

She smiled at him to show she was joking, but Jacob caught the look in her eye. He would try to stay between Abby and Daly if need be.

Jacob hung back, watching for signs of Daly as the

others all filed into the office. The shadowy figure, a small man with a black, wide-brimmed hat pulled over his eyes, still lurked by the corner of the building. The bounty hunter wasn't able to get a good look at him before he ducked back, but he had his suspicions. He didn't like letting that man out of his sight, but Santos needed Jacob inside.

He opened the door and stepped into the cool, dark office.

CHAPTER SIX

The Rockville Mining Company office at the Vernon
Copper Mine in Jasper, Arizona, consisted of one
single large room, divided in half by a partial wall,
partitioning Mr. Farnsworth's office from that of his
secretary. Jacob hung back near the door to take it all
in. The building had just the single door, with a
window on either side. None of the other three walls
offered any way in or out of the room—which could
be good or bad, depending on the situation. Jacob
eyed the secretary's desk in front of him, trying to
discern if it had any hidden compartments for
weapons or other defensive mechanisms.

Mr. Farnsworth may trust Floyd Daly, but that
didn't mean Jacob shouldn't be prepared for the day
Daly might turn on him.

Santos had introduced himself and his party to the
secretary, a serious young man who had already found

a way to mention in conversation that he had attended Harvard University. Even though Mr. Farnsworth could clearly hear the entire conversation and was sitting only ten feet away, the secretary behaved as though his boss were in a high tower somewhere else.

"I'm afraid I can't let you speak to Mr. Farnsworth without an appointment."

Santos pulled out his U.S. Marshal badge. "I believe the law always has a standing appointment, young man."

"Humphries, it's fine," Farnsworth grunted from the back of the room. "Send them back. I don't want you to waste more time arguing about it."

Humphries frowned and gestured for the group to cross into the older man's office. Farnsworth stood behind his desk to greet them. He held his pocket watch in hand and glanced at it over and over in between watching the visitors enter.

"I'll give you five minutes," he said, still standing.

"I appreciate you taking the time, Mr. Farnsworth," Santos began.

"Get on with it," the mining official said.

"I understand you have a man in your employment by the name of Floyd Daly."

"This again?" Farnsworth plopped into his chair and put his feet on his desk. "I already told Sheriff Alway that he has the wrong man. Floyd Daly must be a very popular name. There's no way my man is the thief and murderer Alway has described."

"I think we can clear that up pretty easily, Mr. Farnsworth," Jacob said. "As U.S. Marshal, Mr. Santos has the wanted poster asking for Floyd Daly's arrest, which of course includes an illustration which might help clear up your confusion. I'm surprised Sheriff Alway didn't show you his copy of it."

"Oh, he tried to, at first. But I don't believe it. Mr. Daly has increased production here by nearly three hundred percent."

He paused to let that number sink in. Jacob didn't want to think about what Daly had done or threatened to do in order to get that number.

"That may be, Mr. Farnsworth," Jacob said. "But we have reason to believe your employee has a demonstrated pattern of behavior that indicates he will steal from the company or cheat you directly. We'd like to take him into custody before that happens—if it hasn't already."

"Oh, you say you're looking out for me, do you? I don't believe it. I don't want to hear it." Farnsworth looked up from his pocket watch and frowned at the crowd that had invaded his office. "I believe your five minutes is up."

"Mr. Farnsworth." Abby stepped out from the group of men and fluttered her eyelashes at the mining executive. Jacob noticed that she had banished all sounds of anger or frustration from her voice. "You must be a very smart man to have hired such a productive new employee. Especially seeing as he probably doesn't even have mining experience."

He eyed her warily. "Yes, I think so . . ."

"I am a business woman myself," she said, placing a delicate hand to her bosom. "I try to make as smart of hires as I can, and I certainly am always careful to keep my best employees happy."

"What kind of business do you run, miss?"

"But at the same time," she continued, ignoring his question, "I understand that I cannot possibly know every little thing that goes on in my business. That's when I'm grateful to get other people's opinions."

Mr. Farnsworth exhaled a groan.

"For example, Mr. Devlin here." She gestured to the neatly dressed man standing on her left. "He has had many interactions with Floyd Daly, and each of them has left him poorer than the last."

After a moment of silence, she elbowed Devlin in the side, prodding him forward.

"Ahem." He cleared his throat. "That's right. Mr. Daly was a customer of mine since he moved to Jasper, but—"

"But can you really call him a *customer*," Abby interrupted, "if he has never paid his bills?"

"That's right." Devlin nodded, Abby's confidence seeming to bolster his own. "Mr. Daly opened a credit account at my store—using his job at your own company as collateral, Mr. Farnsworth. But he has yet to pay a single dime of what he owes me."

"You want me to pay his bills, is that it?" Farnsworth asked, pulling out his money clip. He peeled a bill off the top and tossed it across the desk.

The bill floated to the ground at Devlin's feet. He looked confused, but bent to pick it up. "No, I—"

"He owes *me* money, too," Gentle Jack shouted.

"Mr. Farnsworth, we seem to have lost the thread here." Santos spoke soothingly, trying to regain control of the conversation. "These fine citizens are all here to testify about how they have been wronged by the man currently in your employ. If you could tell us where to find him, so that we may apprehend him in accordance with the law, we hope to stop him from wronging you or your company."

Farnsworth stood again, this time coming around his desk. Jacob hoped for a short moment that they had gotten through to him, despite what his gut was telling him.

"Your five minutes was up long ago, and I have been more than polite. The only ones costing me or Rockville Mining Company money are you lot, so I'll see you out. Good day."

Even with five people in their group, unless Santos indicated they should get violent and physical with Mr. Farnsworth, there was nothing they could do. Without Daly anywhere in the room, there was no call for the law to do anything other than leave the company in peace.

Jacob waited to exit last, still looking for that one hint that would indicate that Farnsworth and Humphries were ready for whatever might befall them, but the solid walls of wooden planks looked bare.

CHAPTER SEVEN

"Now what do we do?" Abby demanded as they stepped out of the mining office.

Devlin still held the twenty-dollar bill loosely in his hand. Abby snatched it from him.

"We are all owed money," she said, before he could object. "If this is all we're getting, we'll have to split it."

"He owes me money, too," Gentle Jack said—again practically shouting the words.

Santos tried to calm them down, but Abby and Jack were already yelling at each other.

Jacob inched around to the side of the building where he had seen the man watching them earlier. None of the other workers came over to this corner; it was farthest away from the mine and the water supply, and there were no entrances to the office on that side.

The bounty hunter approached cautiously, his hand on his grip.

The shade of a nearby tree hit this side of the building, creating a curtain of dappled shadow that made it difficult for Jacob to immediately identify any footprints or other possible clues. He stopped to listen, but the bustling and arguing of the group behind him was too distracting. He sniffed, checking to see if he could smell an unwashed outlaw, but no aroma stood out to his keen nose.

Five more steps brought Jacob around the corner of the office, but there was no one skulking around here either, and as far as he could see, there were no clues or indications of where the man had gone.

It had to have been Daly, though. Jacob could not think of any other reason a man would sneak around watching a U.S. Marshal and his deputy unless that man was a wanted outlaw. All this meant Daly was likely somewhere nearby. He wasn't in the office, nor was he around the office anymore.

Jacob turned around and strode off to the mouth of the Vernon Copper Mine.

This early in the day, there were only a handful of cars full of ore above ground. Men covered in a thin coat of dirt, hats pulled low over their eyes pushed past Jacob to go down into the shaft. He hesitated; confronting and trying to capture the outlaw in the dark mine could put all of these other workers at risk.

He eyed each man he passed, trying to see if one of them might be Daly.

If a man wanted to hide, the deep, dark reaches of a mine might be a good place to do it. Jacob was sure that he'd find the man in this pit if he looked hard enough.

He ignored the questioning looks a few of the miners shot at him. There was no time to explain. Daly could already be deep in the recesses. Jacob crossed into the mouth of the hole, pausing only a moment to let his eyes adjust to the darkness. The banging, tumbling rock, and shouting orders were louder in here. He couldn't cease all production, so he'd just have to do a visual search. In the dark.

Jacob took a deep breath and began his descent.

Twenty yards into the mine, a mancart stood waiting to ferry workers farther down. Jacob briefly tried to explain to the man in charge what he was doing here, but the worker didn't seem to care. He just ushered Jacob into the cart with the other men and transferred him down to the next level. Once farther below, the workers scattered, leaving Jacob to wonder which way to go.

Before the last of the miners disappeared into the darkness out of his sight, Jacob stopped him, grabbing his arm.

"Where can I find Daly?"

"Shoot, I don't know, mister."

"Guess."

"I'm not sure I should."

"I've got a deputy U.S. Marshal badge that says you should."

"All right, all right." The miner shook off Jacob's grip. "No need to threaten. Daly could be anywhere, really. He seems to have a finger in every pie."

"But if you had to pick?" Jacob was getting impatient.

"If I had to pick . . . well, lately Daly's been spending more time in the older shafts. Down that way." He pointed to the shaft behind Jacob and to the left. "There aren't many still working that shaft, though. You'd better take a candle with you."

"Thanks."

"Be careful. That flame burns too much, you're liable to lose your breath."

"I got it."

Jacob grabbed one of the last candles that rested on a table at the foot of the cart track and lit it, holding it carefully in front of him. Anyone who came down later would just be out of luck.

As he started down the shaft the miner had indicated, Jacob unholstered his revolver. He would prefer to take Daly without any bloodshed, but he knew that wasn't always possible. He held the candle up in front of him. The flickering light, combined with the rock walls around him, cast harsh shadows. Twice Jacob went to turn down another branch of tunnel only to find out it was simply a depression in the wall, filled with darkness.

After thirty yards of cautious progress, Jacob still had not run into any other workers. This really was an abandoned shaft of the Vernon Copper Mine. If he did come across Daly down here, and things went south, who knew how long it would be before anyone else came down here.

Jacob thought he heard some kind of shuffling. It could be a rat, bat, or other creature, but he paused to listen more carefully. Somewhere near him—maybe just around that next turn in the tunnel—was *something*.

Something alive. Something moving.

He took another few steps toward the sound. He held his breath, not wanting to give anything away. Now he was almost sure those were footsteps. It sounded like heavy boots on the mine's rock floor.

He took another three steps, just reaching the turn in the tunnel.

A swift breath blew out his candle flame.

In the darkness, Jacob heard the click of a hammer being pulled back.

He inched toward the sound, but before he could relight his candle, the crack of gunshot echoed through the chamber.

CHAPTER EIGHT

The dirt wall behind Jacob exploded where the bullet hit, just inches to his left but fortunately missing him. The shot had been fired from relatively close by—his ears rang from the blast. The ringing began to fade, and the first noise Jacob could identify was footsteps running deeper into the mine, away from him.

That was too close. And if Jacob had been shot, he would never have made it out of here. Trying to capture Daly while inside the mine was too big of a risk. Jacob kicked the rock wall in frustration and made his way back up to the surface, leaving Daly to his dark hidey-hole.

As he returned to the daylight, Jacob did his best to avoid running into any miners. He had been deep underground, but that didn't mean the sound of a gunshot had gone unnoticed.

When he emerged back into the light, he noticed

Santos and the group still waiting for him. The marshal sat atop his horse, eyes scanning the horizon in all directions. When his gaze fell on Jacob, the other man's shoulders visibly relaxed.

"Payne!"

He dismounted and hurried over to where Jacob was exiting the mine. As he got closer, Jacob realized how much he must have worried Santos. The man was frowning and reaching out to grab Jacob as soon as he was close enough.

"What happened? Where did you go? I thought I heard a gunshot, but I wasn't sure. I don't like the idea of us splitting up." Santos began brushing dirt off Jacob's sleeve. He hadn't realized how much the exploding wall had hit him in the dark.

"He almost shot me," Jacob said. "In the dark. Daly shot at me. I didn't even know he was there. We've got to come up with a better plan."

Santos nodded soberly. "Let's head back to Jasper and reassess."

Jacob started toward the horses, but the marshal stopped him.

"It'll be easier to do this once we no longer have the whole gang with us," Santos said in a whisper.

Jacob nodded and made his way to where Yellow stood, patiently waiting for him.

"You okay?" Abby asked cautiously.

"Fit as a fiddle," he said. "The man surprised me in

the dark, but it takes more than a shock to take down Jacob Payne."

Abby laughed at his bravado. "All right, Mr. Payne. Just don't you go dying on me before we get justice, ya hear?"

"Wouldn't think of it." He climbed on his horse, taking the reins from the miner who had untied Yellow for him.

"We all ready?" Santos asked the group.

Among a chorus of yeses, the marshal led them back up the road to town. He rode ahead, listening to Gentle Jack rant and rave angrily about all the injustices done him. Jacob didn't hear everything he said, but caught the general idea. He was happy to trail in the back of the group, making sure no one got separated but also able to have a private conversation with Abby.

"How long have you lived in Jasper?" he asked her.

She smiled and flashed a dimple at him. "Why? You thinking about staying around?"

He chuckled. "No, nothing like that. Just wondering what brought you here."

Her smile grew strained, but she didn't give any other indication she was distressed by his question. All she said was, "I came here a couple years ago. From South Carolina."

"Really? I thought I heard some southern in that accent of yours."

"Yes, sir. After the war a lot of things changed in

our hometown, so we lit on out of there to look for a new chance somewhere else."

Jacob almost didn't want to ask the next question, didn't want to seem like he was prying. But he asked anyway. "We?"

They rode in silence for a minute or two. Jacob wasn't even sure she had heard his question until she looked at him again. She didn't say a word, but just from her set jaw and pained expression he could tell his question had struck a nerve.

"How exactly were you cheated by Floyd Daly?" Jacob asked quietly.

The look she shot him broke his heart. She was trying to be so strong and so brave, but he could tell that Daly had really hurt her. She bit her lip, as though thinking, but they were already to her hotel. Abby dismounted and handed her horse's reins over to her stable boy, who had been waiting for her. She went inside, not say anything more to Jacob.

CHAPTER NINE

Abby's stable boy offered to take care of Jacob's and Santos's horses as well, and Jacob gratefully handed over his reins. He wanted to hurry inside to finish his conversation. What had happened to this poor woman to make her so angry? How exactly had Floyd Daly hurt her?

When he stepped inside, Jacob looked everywhere before finally noticing Abby sitting alone in the corner of her saloon. It was just about lunchtime, but since most of the men in Jasper worked at the mine, business was slow. The room was quiet.

Santos noticed Abby about the same time and elbowed Jacob forward.

"You go," he said in a low tone. "I'll get us food. I get the feeling she doesn't want to be crowded."

Jacob nodded, removing his hat and crossing the

room. As he reached Abby's table, one of her waitresses brought a glass of beer and set it down in front of her.

"Can I get you one, Mr. Payne?"

"Coffee?"

The waitress nodded and left.

"You not drinking with me, Jacob?" Abby smiled at him, but he could tell her heart wasn't in her teasing.

He reached across the table and put his hand over hers. "What happened, Abby?"

She withdrew her hand from his and scooted her chair away—only a couple inches, but enough for him to notice. She kept her eyes on him while she gulped back several large swallows of beer. He returned his hands to his lap and waited. She would tell him when she was ready, or she would leave. He didn't want to force her.

The waitress returned with his coffee. He thanked her, and once she left again Jacob and Abby sat in silence for nearly a minute. Jacob was debating whether or not to get up and leave her alone when she finally spoke.

"I haven't told you how I came by this place, have I?"

"No, ma'am."

She nodded and drained her beer before speaking again.

"I came out west with my husband and his brother two years ago. My husband had been diagnosed with consumption, and the doctor told us the dry air in the west would be the best treatment. My brother-in-law had a hankering for space and a change, so he came with us."

Jacob couldn't see where this was leading, or what this had to do with Floyd Daly, but he stayed quiet, sipping his coffee as he listened.

"It's a good thing he did come with us, since my husband—his name was Jacob, too, if you'll believe it —he died while we were still in Texas. He never even made it to Arizona. Joseph and me stayed to bury him, and I suppose I could have gone back to South Carolina, but I wanted to see it all the way to the end. So Joseph and me kept on till we landed here in Jasper. Two years ago, like I said.

"It was hard when we first got here. Joseph tried out mining and I kept house, and we went on like that for a few months. But . . ."

She trailed off and looked out toward the window. An older man driving a cart proceeded down the road. Jacob took the moment of Abby's distraction as a chance to glance behind him. Santos was leaning on the bar, watching them from a distance.

"Joseph had an accident in the mine," Abby began, and Jacob turned his attention back to her. "I still don't know how it happened, but one of his legs was crushed. Doc Jewett amputated it in time to save his life, but he couldn't work there anymore. We were . . . there never was anything between Joseph and me. He was like my brother, above anything. But still. I couldn't leave him. He was my family, and we were stuck out here in the hills of Arizona with no job, no way to take care of ourselves."

Her eyes had glazed over while she spoke. Jacob was silent.

"Bad luck following bad luck, it was . . . but I guess God done thought we'd had enough. This here hotel came up for sale, and the owner knew we had little else to do and sold it to us for a deal. His wife had died, and I had filled in as cook and maid a couple times for him, and he wanted to go back east. So I gave him everything. All our savings, all my jewelry—my husband's gun, even. That gun had made me feel safe for a year since he'd died, but it was worth trading for a chance at having a real life."

"So it seems like you've done well for yourself," Jacob ventured.

Abby finally met his eyes.

"Right about the time that the hotel was turned over to Joseph and me, Floyd Daly showed up in town."

"Oh."

"I didn't pay him no mind, at first. He even paid his bill for the two weeks he stayed here as a hotel guest. I didn't have any hint of what he was capable of. At first."

She sighed and took another swallow of beer.

"But then, I started to notice Joseph was more

and more agitated. He would yell at me for the smallest thing, like throwing away a batch of biscuits that hadn't turned out right, or when I bought more soap than he thought we needed. I couldn't understand why he was so stressed. The hotel was doing good business, so far as I knew. But then one night, Joseph finally cracked under all that pressure. He told me he'd had to borrow money to pay for a share in another mine some fellas were trying to open, and for the new wallpaper upstairs we'd installed recently. He told me this Daly guy had promised to be understanding and would set a reasonable interest, but that he hadn't been able to pay him back fast enough."

Abby paused, letting that sink in.

"I asked him, 'What do we owe?' But he couldn't —he wouldn't—say. Joseph Courtland—this man who had been my brother in all but blood, who I had loved dearly for years—had gone behind my back and . . ."

She buried her face in her hands, elbows leaning on the table. Jacob was shocked. This woman sitting before him had shown such strength and poise; he never would have guessed she was suffering so much.

"Joseph had promised Daly he could have *me*," she whispered into her hands. "I didn't want to agree to it. I threw things and hit Joseph until I had no more strength in me, but it didn't do any good. He just took all of it, because he knew there was no other option. If I didn't go along with the plan, Daly could take the hotel from us. It wasn't until after that awful night that I learned what Joseph had traded me for."

"What?" Jacob asked quietly.

She looked up at him with a wry smile, her eyes rimmed red. "A month's extension. Not in exchange for the money that was owed, or even a portion of the money. No, all Joseph deemed my virtue to be worth was a few extra weeks to come up with the money."

She released a sad, choking laugh.

"Joseph died before that month was even up. I guess he had been hiding his own consumption diagnosis for awhile." She shook her head, amazed. "He's lucky he did, or I might have killed him myself. His life insurance paid off Daly, and I've made my choices in the months since. I take in the girls who have been in my situation, and I help them take care of themselves when no one else will. But that devil won't ever let me forget what he held over us. Over me. He's constantly needling me, offering to pay more for 'another go.'"

"Abby . . ." Jacob risked it again: he cautiously reached across the table to take her hand, and this time she didn't withdraw. Angry tears sprung from her eyes. Tears he wished he could brush away. "We *will* get Floyd Daly. I promise you that. At the very least, he will be behind bars. And I will do everything in my power to make sure you are compensated for what he has cheated you out of, if such a thing can be compensated."

She nodded, but before she could respond, the door banged open and a dirt-covered miner burst into the saloon.

"He's done it," the man gasped out, leaning against the doorframe. "Daly. He's attacked."

CHAPTER TEN

Santos was on the man in a second. Jacob rushed to his side, almost upsetting a chair on his way. He looked back at Abby, but she waved him on. In the moment of crisis, her tough, invulnerable exterior had returned.

"Who has he attacked? What's going on?" Santos demanded.

The miner caught his breath. "Daly snapped. I don't know why. I didn't see it. They sent me here to get you."

"All right. We're going."

Jacob ran out the door of the hotel and down the street to the next block, where their horses were just getting brushed down in the livery. He shouted out commands, saddling as he went, and was able to get their horses out and ready in record time. He leapt onto Yellow and led Santos's horse back to the hotel.

In the few minutes he had been gone, the marshal had managed to dig more details out of the messenger from the mining company.

"Seems there was an explosion down in the mine and while everyone was looking that way, Daly used the distraction to take control of the mining office."

"That bastard," Jacob said.

"We'll get him," Santos assured him. "Abby!" The hotel proprietress was in the doorway, watching them get ready to leave. "Send word to Sheriff Alway, will you? Tell him I want him on the scene."

"You think he'll go?"

"I trust you can make the situation clear to him," he said with a smile.

She nodded, and that was the last thing they saw before they galloped down the road back toward the mine. Moving this fast, their approach took less time than earlier in the morning. The scene at the mine was still chaos, with injured men being carried out of the mineshaft and another crowd of armed men gathering around the office.

"Where is he?" Jacob demanded as they approached.

Two of the workers came forward to take charge of their horses while three others gathered around, all talking at once and relaying the events of the last hour.

"No one saw him go in," the first one said.

"We still don't know how the explosion happened," said the second.

"It was Daly," the third replied. Jacob recognized him as the man who had given him directions in the mine earlier. "I done told you Daly's rotten—*he* set the blast!"

"Okay, fellas, calm down," Santos said in his low, soothing tone. "What matters most is we make sure everyone is safe now. Where is Daly?"

All three men pointed to the office building. Now that they were closer, Jacob noticed that both of the front windows looked to have big wooden boards behind them. There was no clear line of sight into the office.

"Those look like the bookshelves, pushed in front of the window," Santos said. "He's barricaded himself in there. We'll have to figure out how to draw him out."

"We don't know yet what kind of weapons the man has," Jacob said. "Maybe we can find Humphries. He must have known the man."

The sound of horses drew Jacob's attention. Coming down the road, leading a group of half a dozen others, came Abby Courtland. She looked determined. When they got close enough, Jacob noticed that she had another horse tied to her own and was guiding it along with her.

Riding the ponying horse was Sheriff Alway.

Jacob almost laughed at the pained expression on the man's face, but shook his head instead. The man was supposed to be the law in this town. He was the one should be bringing justice to Jasper, Arizona.

Also following Abby were Gentle Jack, Mr. Devlin, and five other townspeople she had somehow managed to gather for the event. Whatever Santos needed to defuse this situation, they had plenty of help on their side.

"Let me talk to Mr. Farnsworth," Santos said. "I need to find out what all is in that office that could be used as a weapon."

Jacob's mind went to those desk drawers he never got to check.

"You can't," the miner said. "Farnsworth is in there. Humphries, too. Daly has taken them hostage."

Santos looked stricken. They already knew Daly was a man who would sacrifice other people for his own gain. Looked like their warning to Farnsworth had come to pass.

"Hostage?" Jacob asked. "What is he demanding?"

The miner shook his head. "Money. Lots of money."

"Damn," Santos cursed under his breath.

"I've got an idea," Jacob said. "You just keep his focus on you."

Santos seemed to catch on quick. "If we can keep him talking, he won't have time to shoot anyone."

"I'm going to find another way in," Jacob said.

The marshal nodded and turned his full body to the office building.

"Come out of there, Daly!" Santos yelled. "This won't end well for you!"

CHAPTER ELEVEN

Jacob left Santos shouting at the Rockville Mining Company office and ducked around the corner of the building, where he'd spotted Daly at their first visit to the office. One benefit of Daly having pushed the bookshelves up against the front windows was he wouldn't be able to see where Jacob had gone.

The bounty hunter wondered what the outlaw was doing in there. Robbing Farnsworth? Robbing the entire company? Jacob had noticed the safe in the corner of Farnsworth's office. It was possible it held the pay for the hundreds of men who worked there. A nice haul for a man like Daly.

He stood close to the building and heard a low thrum of talking from inside. The walls were thin— just a handful of pine boards nailed to the frame. He couldn't hear what was said, but there little enough between Jacob and the men on the other side of the wall that he knew when they were speaking and even where they were standing.

There must be some way he could use that knowledge to his advantage.

Jacob stayed close to the wall, listening, stepping gently so they couldn't hear him too. If Daly was smart, he'd be worried about the fact that he had no line of vision out of the office. But from all the stories Jacob hard heard so far that day, it sounded more like Daly was impulsive than careful. It could have been anything that led him to break his calm facade today rather than any other day.

As he made his way around the back of the office, Jacob realized this was nearest to where Daly must be standing. His voice was noticeably higher than either Farnsworth's or Humphries's, and that voice was louder through the thin wall in the back.

As he watched, the wall itself bowed out a little toward him. He paused, stepping back and watching. His best guess was that Daly, or one of the others, must be leaning against the wall there. The office had been thrown up in a hurry and didn't have the structural strength to hold a grown man's weight. After a minute, Daly must have stood up again because the wall went straight. Jacob crept up to take a closer look.

The corner, where the end of the plank connected to the frame, was ever so slightly coming loose. Not more than a quarter of an inch, but the nails were not holding. If Daly were to lean on the wall again, the board and maybe even the entire wall would come apart.

This was the in Jacob had been waiting for.

He pulled his Bowie knife out of his boot and carefully inserted the sharp point into the gap by the nail. He would have to go slowly and quietly, so as to not draw Daly's attention. The outlaw would be holding at least one weapon, maybe more, and if Daly thought there was a possible threat on the other side of this wall, he wouldn't hesitate to shoot.

The bounty hunter maneuvered his knife deeper into the gap. He had chosen a spot between the two nails and would soon have the knife far enough in the gap to leverage and widen it.

Just before he was about to tilt his knife up and pry off the board, the weight again fell against the wall. Jacob jumped back and around the corner, letting go of his knife. With Daly's weight again against the wall, the nails fell out even more, pushing the gap in the wall to half an inch.

Jacob could see light through the gap. It was wide enough that he could see the color of the shirt Daly was wearing. Which meant, if the outlaw thought to look, he would be able to see Jacob outside. Jacob held his breath, waiting for him to walk away again.

"That marshal is stupid." The voice Jacob heard didn't sound like Farnsworth or Humphries. He heard the *thud* of something hit the floor near where he stood, maybe the butt of a rifle or shotgun. "He thinks he can just *talk* me into giving myself up?"

Jacob was incensed. Not only was this outlaw a bully, thief, and manipulator, but he had the gall to insult the law as well. He would take great pleasure in bringing this man down.

Daly stood up again and his footsteps on the wooden floorboards told Jacob when he was six feet and then ten feet away. He hurriedly picked up his knife from the ground and again set to work prying the board free of its frame.

He left the board where it was and pulled out the nails on the end closest to him. It balanced precariously, sitting on top of the plank below it. Jacob pulled the board away from the frame to peek inside.

What he saw infuriated him.

Directly across the room from Jacob, Farnsworth and Humphries sat in two small chairs. Daly hadn't even bothered to tie them up, so sure was he that his gun would keep them in line. But, seeing as neither of the other men had weapons or any means of defense, it seemed to have been a pretty good gamble.

Farnsworth caught his glance and widened his eyes. Jacob shook his head, silently pleading with the other man to be quiet. He seemed to know what was needed and called to Daly, drawing attention to himself.

"How else are you gonna get the money you asked for, then, if you don't go out there?"

"I dunno," the outlaw said sullenly. "They'll bring it in here."

"You sure that's all you want, Daly? Just money to get out of town? Seems a bit amateur for a man like you."

"Shut up, old man. You don't know what you're talking about."

"I know there are some people in this town you have pissed off mightily. They're probably all out there right now." Farnsworth pointed at the door. "How're you planning on getting through that crowd."

Throughout this conversation, Jacob pried off the board as quickly and quietly as possible. Farnsworth did a good job of not looking at him over Daly's shoulder, and of keeping his voice raised to disguise any sounds Jacob might be making. Directing his attention to the front of the office was good thinking on his part.

Humphries kept looking at Jacob, but fortunately Daly wasn't paying any attention to him.

"They'll be through that front door any minute," Farnsworth said. "You'd better have a plan."

"They'll not take me," Daly said. He lifted his shotgun up halfheartedly as he backed up toward the corner where Jacob peered in. "I'll see any man come through that door and blast his head off."

"So you think you're going to shoot your way out?" Farnsworth said.

"You got a better idea?" Daly shot back. He slowly

moved to lean back against the wall again, near Jacob's corner.

The bounty hunter saw his chance.

Jacob held his breath and pushed his revolver through the gap in the boards.

CHAPTER TWELVE

"Stop right there," Jacob said in a menacing tone.

His revolver was jabbed into the ribs of Floyd Daly.

The outlaw tried to turn his head to see who had stopped him.

"What the—"

"I said stop," Jacob commanded.

With his right hand holding his revolver steady, Jacob used his left hand to rip off more of the planks creating the back wall of the office. Farnsworth groaned at the destruction, but didn't protest. In just a few seconds, Jacob had created a gap big enough for him to step through without removing his gun from Daly's side.

This was the first time Jacob had gotten a good look at the man, but even from behind it was clearly Floyd Daly. He matched the description from the wanted poster perfectly—long dirty blond hair, scraggily dirty blond beard, and only a couple inches taller than five feet.

"This is what we're going to do," Jacob said. "I'm going to count to three. You're going to put your shotgun on the desk with the barrel pointed away from the other men. If you move before I say three, you're dead. If you try to shoot that gun, you're dead. If you dare set the shotgun down in any place or any manner other than what I have specifically told you to do, you're dead. Let me hear you say you understand."

There was a tense moment of almost guttural growling from Daly before Jacob heard him say, "I understand."

"All right, then. One . . . two . . . three."

Jacob moved forward with the outlaw the few inches he needed to lean to set the gun down, his revolver never leaving the other man's side.

"Okay, then. Do you have any other weapons I need to know about?"

"No."

"He's lying," Farnsworth said, almost sounding bored by it. "Of course he does."

"Where?" Jacob demanded.

"Meddling whoremonger—" Daly began.

"Where is it?"

Daly shut his mouth, then said, "I have a derringer tucked into the back of my pants."

Even before he finished the sentence, Jacob had fished the small gun out. "Anything else?"

"A Bowie knife in my right boot," he said through clenched teeth.

"Well, what do you know?" said Jacob. "So do I."

He tucked the derringer into his jacket pocket and stooped to pull the knife out of Daly's boot.

"Are we done?" Jacob asked. "I'm sure you can guess what will happen if I find you've been holding anything back."

"We're done," Daly said petulantly.

"Wonderful. Mr. Humphries," Jacob said to the trembling young man. "Would you please go outside and inform the U.S. Marshal that Floyd Daly has been apprehended?"

He nodded vigorously and all but ran to the front door of the office.

"How are you feeling, Mr. Farnsworth?"

The older man had moved from the chair and was seated against the far wall of the office, arms crossed over his chest. "You certain you have that weasel under control?"

"Yes, sir. There's no reason to be afraid."

"I'm not afraid," he boomed. Farnsworth crossed the room in two strides and began rifling through the outlaw's pockets.

"Hey!" Daly protested.

"I'm taking back what's rightfully mine."

"Can we wait on that, do you think, Mr.

Farnsworth?" Jacob asked. "Seems there are a lot of people in this town owed money—and apologies—from this man."

Farnsworth didn't pause in his search. "I'm sure there are. And I'm sure there'd be fewer victims in Jasper if I had listened to Sheriff Alway the first time. I aim to make sure each and every one of them are paid what they are owed. But that starts with stripping this devil of every penny he has on him."

Jacob shook his head. He'd have to let the marshal sort this out.

At that thought, the door opened and several men filed in, Humphries leading Santos and Alway into the office.

"Sheriff, can you see to this criminal, please?" Santos asked calmly.

"We'll take him back to Tucson tomorrow?" Jacob asked.

The marshal nodded. "He can wait. I'd rather make the trip in one piece. I trust Mrs. Courtland still has a room for us at her establishment."

"I'm hankering for more of that stew," Jacob said, grinning.

As they passed the filthy and muttering outlaw over to the custody of the quivering sheriff, Jacob kept both weapons up, ready in case Daly tried to make a run for it in the confusion.

Farnsworth seized the sheriff by the shoulder. "Alway! You had better keep that man locked up until these men can take him to Tucson. If I hear even the breath of a rumor that he's been freed or lost, I will see to it that you never work in this town again."

"No, sir, Mr. Farnsworth. I won't, sir."

"And you boys." He addressed Santos and Jacob. "When will you need me to testify? I'll *walk* all the way to Tucson if it means seeing this man hanged."

"I'll send word when I know for sure, Mr. Farnsworth. We're not expecting the circuit judge before next week sometime."

"Next week it is, then. I'm grateful to you both. Mighty grateful." He shook both of their hands. "It's a damn shame, though. That man did get my mine producing more than it has in years. And now I need to rebuild my office on top of it all."

"But, Mr. Farnsworth," Jacob said. "Would you want that mine producing if it meant he was stealing from or threatening your workers?"

The man looked thoughtful, shrugged, and said again, "It's a damn shame."

Abby had snuck through the office door and directed two of the miners to move the bookshelves back away from the windows. Despite her long road to get where she was, Abby had the temperament and skills of a born manager. Now, without the threat of Daly, Jacob had no doubt she'd make her hotel into the finest and busiest in all the Territory of Arizona.

"You don't have to leave, do you, Mr. Payne? You sure you don't want to stay?" Abby said, sauntering over to him. "I think Jasper'll be needing a new candidate for sheriff right soon."

"That's mighty kind of you, Mrs. Courtland."

"Abby. Please."

Jacob grinned. "Abby. I'm sure whoever steps into that role will be much obliged for your advice and support. But it'll be enough for me to stay one more night and have supper with you."

ALSO BY A.T. BUTLER

Blood on the Mountain — the fourth adventure in the Jacob Payne series — is now available!

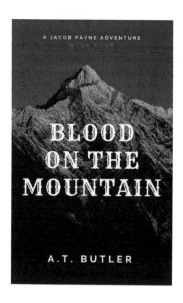

In the mountains of eastern Arizona Territory, bounty hunter Jacob Payne's skills are required to rescue a teenage girl.

Flora Kimball has been kidnapped from her family's farm, right under her father's nose. The neighbors of Elk Springs refuse to help, content to leave her to her fate. When Jacob learns of the tragedy, he teams up with a family friend to go after the outlaw and his captive.

Despite overwhelming odds, a skittish horse, and uncertain allies, Jacob vows to bring this girl home safely and unharmed ...

Blood on the Mountain is fourth in the Jacob Payne series of western novels. Each book is a standalone story. They can be read out of order, but reading experience is enhanced if the series is read consecutively.

———

Jacob Payne Series:

Trouble By Any Name

Danger in the Canyon

Justice for Jasper

Blood on the Mountain

Outlaw Country

Death By Grit

Desert Rage

Arizona Legacy

Fool's Demise

Silent Night

Jacob Payne Box Set: Books 1-3

Jacob Payne Box Set: Books 4-6

Jacob Payne Box Set: Books 7-9

Courage On The Oregon Trail Series:

Westward Courage

Faithful Trail

Frontier Sisters

Unyielding Heart

Other Western Novels by A.T. Butler:

Hawke's Revenge

Loyalty's Price

ABOUT THE AUTHOR

I grew up in the southwest—California Missions, snakes and constant threat of drought weaving the backdrop of my childhood.

But it wasn't until I moved to Texas a few years ago that the magic and mythology of the American West began to seep into my soul.

I'd love to write about Jacob Payne for a long time. ...

If you enjoyed this book, a review on your favorite retailer would be greatly appreciated.

Be sure to sign up for my newsletter for all the updates on future books at atbutler.com/free.

- A

BLOOD ON THE MOUNTAIN - CHAPTER ONE

"Your deal?" Jacob Payne asked as he tossed his cards into the middle of the poker table. This had never been his game and he was tempted to just get up and leave, but couldn't quite resist trying one more time. He, Edwin and two strangers had been playing for a couple hours already and Jacob was still running just about even. One more hand could let him walk away with some real cash.

"Yep," Edwin responded, pulling all the cards toward him.

"This is my last hand," Jacob announced.

There was a short lull while Edwin gathered the deck to shuffle, but no sooner had Jacob breathed a sigh of relief than one of the strangers, the one with the mustache, brought up his complaint again.

"Look, I'm just sayin' ... Them Mormons should stay with their own kind."

"They're not hurting you," Jacob said for what felt like the fortieth time. "The man and his family have a homestead miles away from here, aren't coming to bother you or preach to you. What under the canopy is the actual problem?"

"It's just not right," the man said. He leaned his chair back on just the rear legs so he could reach the spittoon. His gob of yellowy brown saliva fell about an inch short and dribbled down the outside of the metal container. "He's got five wives, I heard. And each one of 'em has a passel of kids. It ain't right."

"Now, how does that work, exactly?" Edwin asked with a grin. "Do the wives all sleep in the same bed? Do they have different rooms? Or do they each get their own house and the fella has to move between each one?"

The mustached stranger—Jacob thought his name was Abe—grimaced. "I don't know," he insisted.

"Did you even meet the man?" Jacob asked.

Abe was speechless for only a moment before sputtering. "I didn't need to *meet* him to know. I heard. And it's not right."

Jacob sighed. It was impossible to argue with someone who didn't have any actual point. "You about ready for that next hand?" he asked Edwin.

The dealer grinned and nodded. The other stranger had remained silent this whole time, but at least his aim with tobacco was better. Jacob eyed him surreptitiously as they played. Abe had called the silent one Lucky, but there was no telling if that was the name he always went by or just one of seven different aliases. As a bounty hunter, Jacob had to keep his suspicions always at the forefront, not taking anything at face value and sinister possibilities everywhere.

Either way, the nickname seemed apt. Lucky had quietly added to his cash over the evening. Jacob didn't always mind losing, but he didn't like seeing one man win that big and that consistently. It took all the fun out of the game.

But he kept his mouth shut.

As the cards landed in front of him, Jacob gently lifted up the corner to see what he had been dealt. Four of spades, Jack of diamonds, three of clubs, nine of diamonds, seven of hearts.

He kept a close eye on the others as they placed their bets. Lucky seemed confident, but Jacob hadn't been playing with them long enough to be able to read any signs of what kinds of cards they may have in front of them.

Going around again, Jacob drew three new cards, keeping his diamonds but not getting anything new worth a damn. Jacob looked at his dwindling cash, and reached a decision. Besides, he didn't want to stick around and listen to more of Abe's griping.

"That's it for me," he said, dropping his cards on the table. "This has been a rich evening, boys."

Abe grinned. "C'mon, stay a bit."

"And give you all more of my money? I don't think so." Jacob clapped Edwin on the shoulder as he passed. "I'll see you tomorrow."

"You off to the cafe?" Edwin asked with a wink.

Jacob paused. He hadn't actually put the idea to himself, but as soon as Edwin mentioned it, he realized that was where he was heading. Having a drink by himself, or maybe in the company of a certain waitress, sounded like the perfect way to end his evening.

"That's what I thought," Edwin said with a laugh when Jacob didn't answer.

"Good night," the bounty hunter said pointedly on his way out the door.

The San Xavier Cafe was only a short block away from the Golden Saddle Saloon where he had been playing. Tucson was growing, and there was even a rumor that they'd get their own newspaper later that fall. Jacob walked purposefully through the dim streets. The sun had just set. The sounds of drinking and the beginnings of evening entertainment surrounded him.

He was getting a little tired of this heat. All the Arizona locals had warned him. He'd laughed it off. But they were right, and he was wrong. His first summer in Arizona had been a shock. When he was on the trail of an outlaw, focused and determined, he could easily ignore the discomfort. On days like this, however, when he was still trying to find a suitable horse to purchase or waiting for a new tip to come in, the heat was all he could think about. It overwhelmed him and influenced every decision.

With the sun below the horizon, the evening was cooler. Jacob took off his hat as he stepped through the door of the San Xavier Cafe and fanned his face a little. He spotted an empty seat at the bar, and was sure to catch the waitress's eye as he sat down.

Bonnie Loft made her way across the room to him with a shy smile. Her dark, almost black, straight hair was pulled back off her face in a low bun, but the tiniest wisps had fallen out to frame her face. Every time she unconsciously reached up to push a strand back behind her ear, he smiled at the gesture.

"I haven't seen you all day, Jacob," she said teasing. "Did you not eat today?"

She ran her small hand across the broad expanse of his back as she crossed behind where he sat. Her touch was casual and fleeting, but Jacob knew she wasn't friendly like this with all her customers.

The old Irish bartender appeared in front of Jacob with a neat whiskey. "Usual, eh, Payne?"

"Thanks, Mickey."

"It breaks my poor heart to see you drinking such dodgy rubbish."

"I know." He grinned. "One day we'll go back to Dublin and you can show me the real stuff."

Justice for Jasper is a work of fiction. Names, characters, places and incidents either are the product of the author's imagination or are used fictitiously. Any resemblance to actual persons living or dead, events or locales is entirely coincidental.

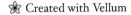 Created with Vellum

Made in the USA
Middletown, DE
15 September 2022

10569936R00052